STORY·MICHAEL ARVAARLUK KUSUGAK
ART·VLADYANA KRYKORKA

Baseball Bats for Christmas

ANNICK PRESS LTD.
TORONTO · NEW YORK · VANCOUVER

©1990 Michael Arvaarluk Kusugak (text)
©1990, 2006 Vladyana Krykorka (art)

Eighth printing, December 2006

Annick Press Ltd.

We acknowledge the support of the Canada Council for the Arts, the Ontario Arts
Council, and the Government of Canada through the Book Publishing Industry
Development Program (BPIDP) for our publishing activities.

Cataloging in Publication Data
    Kusugak, Michael.
      Baseball bats for Christmas

    ISBN 1-55037-145-2 (bound) ISBN 1-55037-144-4 (pbk.)

    I. Krykorka, Vladyana. II. Title

    PS8571.U78B3 1990 jC813'.54 C90-094541-9
    PZ7.K67Ba 1990

Distributed in Canada by: Published in the U.S.A. by Annick Press (U.S.) Ltd.
Firefly Books Ltd.   Distributed in the U.S.A. by:
66 Leek Crescent   Firefly Books (U.S.) Inc.
Richmond Hill, ON   P.O. Box 1338
L4B 1H1   Ellicott Station
                       Buffalo, NY 14205

Printed and bound in Canada by
Friesens, Altona, Manitoba.

visit us at: www.annickpress.com

To my son, Graham Kusugak,
and to Jimi, who read it first
and said, "It's great!"   M.A.K.

To Paul with Love   V.K.

It was a glorious time, even for a very asthmatic boy. Arvaarluk was seven years old, and Arvaarluk was very asthmatic. He struggled when he walked and struggled to catch his breath when he sat down. And Arvaarluk loved Christmas.

In 1955 Arvaarluk lived in Repulse Bay.

Let me tell you a thing or two about Repulse Bay. There is a brass plate on a rock outcrop that was put there when Arvaarluk was just a baby. And no matter how many times you hit it with another rock, it would not come off.

Arvaarluk's mother would say, "If you knock that brass plate off that rock, the whole world will come to a terrible end." Arvaarluk imagined the brass plate coming off and the whole world blowing air out through the hole like a giant seal float bouncing around and around, all over space. So he hit it time and again, but to no avail. It still sits there, declaring for all the world that Repulse Bay is way up at the north end of Hudson Bay—smack dab on the Arctic Circle. Less than one hundred people lived there in 1955 and, in winter, they all lived in igloos and sod huts.

Another thing about Repulse Bay is that there are no "standing-ups." Or, as Peter, Jack, Yvo and Arvaarluk later found out, things commonly known as trees.
There is not one single tree
to be seen anywhere.
The land is as bald as the belly
of a dog with puppies.

In 1955, though, trees arrived in Repulse Bay.
There were six of them.

They came in by aeroplane. As usual, the Union Jack had
been hoisted up the flagpole just before they arrived. The Union
Jack always went up before an aeroplane came. Then Rocky
Parsons flew his trusty Norseman aeroplane over the Arctic
Circle—and ran out of gas. His engine went, "PUTT, PUTT,"
and quit, way up there in the sky. His propeller stopped going
around, but he glided his aeroplane, ever so gracefully, and
plunked it down in front of the Hudson's Bay Company store.
The trees were brought out of the aeroplane and dumped on the
snowbank in front of Arvaarluk's hut. And there they sat.

Rocky Parsons was our hero. When people were sick, he always brought us a doctor. And when we needed stuff he always
came. He appeared in fair weather and foul. All the manager of
the Hudson's Bay Store had to do was hoist up the Union Jack
and Rocky Parsons would come. But we could not talk to Rocky
Parsons because we did not understand any English at all. We
just smiled at him a lot and dreamed of, some day, flying his
aeroplane with him.

Rocky Parsons smiled back as he pumped gas into his
aeroplane from a 45 gallon drum. He pushed and pulled the lever
on his pump back and forth, back and forth, going, "Squish-chuck,
squish-chuck, squish-chuck . . ." Then he jumped back into his
pilot's seat. The Norseman spit out a lot of thick smoke, then
the propeller started going around with such a big "BANG!!!"
that it made your ears dizzy.

He went way out on the ice with the skis bouncing over the
snow drifts going, "Flop, flop, flop, flop . . ." Then, turning
around, he took off with a deafening, "Rooaaarrrr!!!!," just over
their heads. He would not come back until the Union Jack went
up the flagpole again.

But there were the things he had brought sitting on the snowbank in front of Arvaarluk's hut. They were green and had spindly branches all over.

"What are they?" Jack asked.

"Standing-ups," Peter said, confidently. "I have seen them in books at the church. Father Didier showed them to us."

"What are they for?" Yvo asked.

Peter shrugged his shoulders and replied, "I don't know."

They did not have too long to wonder about them, of course. Christmas was coming. There were things to be done. There was church to go to at midnight.

Everyone gathered at the little mission. The older people sat on benches against the walls. The younger men and women stood. And the kids played on the floor in the middle. It was warm and there were electric lights; the only electric lights in all of Repulse Bay. On the walls were pictures of the Pope, the Bishop and Queen Elizabeth. Also on one wall hung a giant pendulum clock. Father Didier, a tall thin man in a black robe, stood with the men and women, smoking his pipe. Around his neck he carried, by a string, a silver cross with Jesus nailed to it. He was a kind man who enjoyed a good laugh. He was our priest, he was our teacher and, when we were sick, he was our nurse.

When the clock chimed midnight, the curtains in front of the church were opened, the benches were rearranged to face the altar and the people sat; women and girls on the left, men and boys on the right. Arvaarluk sat with his mother. Father Didier donned a white, pleated robe and, over that, a fancy vestment with a cross on the back of it. Peter, who was the altar boy, put on a white robe with white lace on the hems. And the service began.

There was a big organ in the church with giant foot pedals and lots of buttons. Father Didier adjusted the buttons, pumped the pedals and played, swaying back and forth as he moved his fingers over the keys. The music filled the small church and people sang:

> O come all ye faithful
> Joyful and triumphant
> O come ye, o come ye
> To Bethlehem.

And so Christmas came.

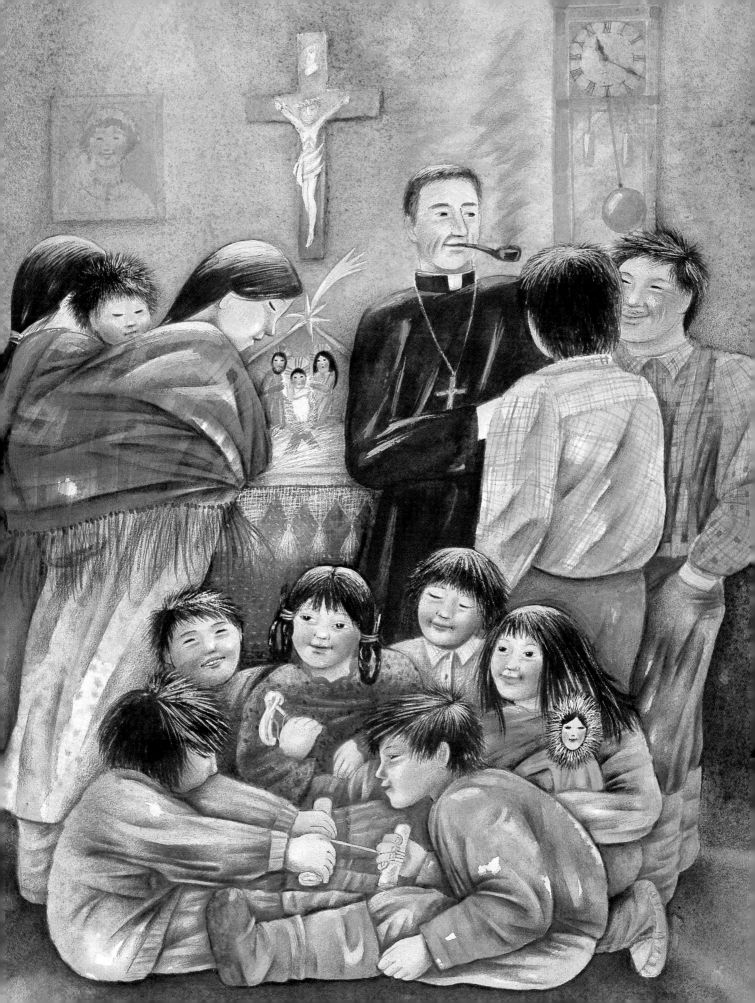

Christmas was a time when you took your most favourite thing in the world and gave it to your very best friend. Arvaarluk trudged in to Peter's igloo with his toy gun (the one with the bullets that looked like real bullets) behind his back. He said, "Happy Nuuya," gave the gun to Peter and left. Peter "Happy Nuuyaed" him a pair of caribou-skin mitts which he wore until the palms had no fur at all left on them—and they were still warm.

Arvaarluk's father gave his only telescope and got a wild dog in return. The dog ran away for a whole year, then came back the following Christmas. But no matter how hard they tried, they could not catch her. When all else failed, Arvaarluk's father lay on his belly on the roof of their hut with a lasso in his hand and waited. When the dog approached the bait he had set, he rose and, twirling the lasso around his head, he threw it.

The lasso flew way out and landed right around the dog's head. The hours and hours Arvaarluk's father had spent playing cowboy had paid off. When they finally tamed it, that dog became the best lead dog they ever had.

That Christmas the manager of the Hudson's Bay Company store gave Arvaarluk a blue and red rubber ball with a white stripe around the middle. We loved to play ball. We would set up four bases, try to find a stick to use for a bat and play. If you had a good stick you could hit the ball a long way. Yvo was the best hitter. He was always the biggest and strongest.

But there are no trees in Repulse Bay and when there are no trees, there are hardly ever any sticks to use for bats. At Christmas in 1955, though, there were trees in Repulse Bay. There were six of them.

Yvo (who was also the smartest) looked at those spindly trees with a twinkle in his eye and said, "I know what those things are for!"

"What?" we all asked.

"Baseball bats," he replied. "Rocky Parsons brought us baseball bats for Christmas."

He got an axe. He took one of the spindly trees and chopped off all spindly branches. Then he fashioned a bat, a real round bat. After much hacking and swinging of the bat to see how it felt, it was ready.

When the kids in Repulse Bay found out about our bat, they all came to play. Yvo batted first with Peter pitching and Arvaarluk playing catcher. Arvaarluk always played catcher since he could not run as much as the other kids. When Yvo hit the ball, it went up far, far away.

"Yay, yay, yay, yay!!!" Everyone cheered, jumping up and down.

Sometimes, when he hit the ball just right, even Arvaarluk could run all the way around and touch all four bases before Jack had time to get the ball and hit him with it to take him out. He would then sit on the fourth base and puff and cough and try to catch his breath. And he would smile and laugh and laugh.

We played ball all that spring and all that summer, making more bats with the spindly trees when they broke. And, in autumn, we could hardly wait for Christmas when, again, the Union Jack would go up the flagpole and Rocky Parsons would, once again, bring us baseball bats for Christmas.

Taima!